OCT   2018

Marvelous
Maravilloso

To my children, Lilia and Leo. May you always see how beautiful you are,
and the colorful beauty in life all around you. I love you!—*CL*

To Wonder-Mela! So thankful for your trust and inspired advice!—*CB*

Published by
MAGINATION PRESS ®
American Psychological Association
750 First Street NE
Washington, DC 20002

Magination Press is a registered trademark of the American Psychological Association.

For more information about our books, including a complete catalog, please write to us,
call 1-800-374-2721, or visit our website at www.apa.org/pubs/magination.

Book design by Sandra Kimbell
Printed by Worzalla, Stevens Point, WI

Library of Congress Cataloging-in-Publication Data
Names: Lara, Carrie, author. | Battuz, Christine, illustrator.
Title: Marvelous Maravilloso : me and my beautiful family / by Carrie Lara ;
   illustrated by Christine Battuz.
Description: Washington, DC : Magination Press, [2018]
Identifiers: LCCN 2017032664| ISBN 9781433828560 (hardcover) |
   ISBN 1433828561 (hardcover)
Subjects: LCSH: Racially mixed children—Juvenile literature.
Classification: LCC HQ777.9 .L37 2018 | DDC 305.8/05--dc23
LC record available at https://lccn.loc.gov/2017032664

Manufactured in the United States of America
10 9 8 7 6 5 4 3 2 1

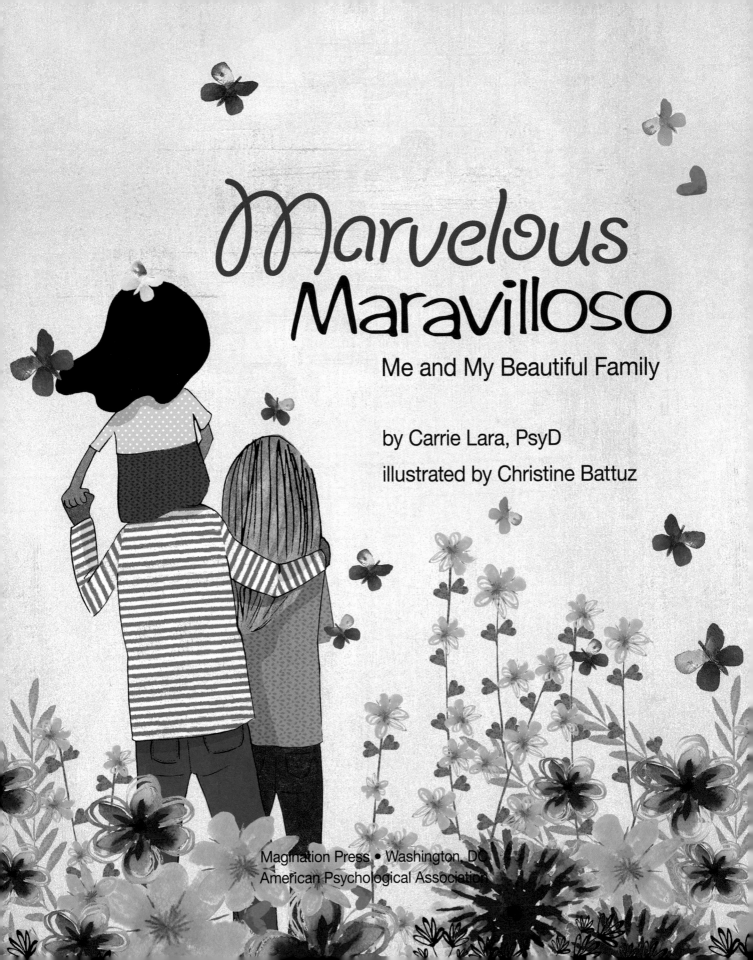

Marvelous
Maravilloso

Me and My Beautiful Family

by Carrie Lara, PsyD

illustrated by Christine Battuz

Magination Press • Washington, DC
American Psychological Association

The world is full of different colors...
hundreds of colors, everywhere.

Mommy and Daddy and I go for walks in the garden to see the rainbow of colors in las flores—the flowers.

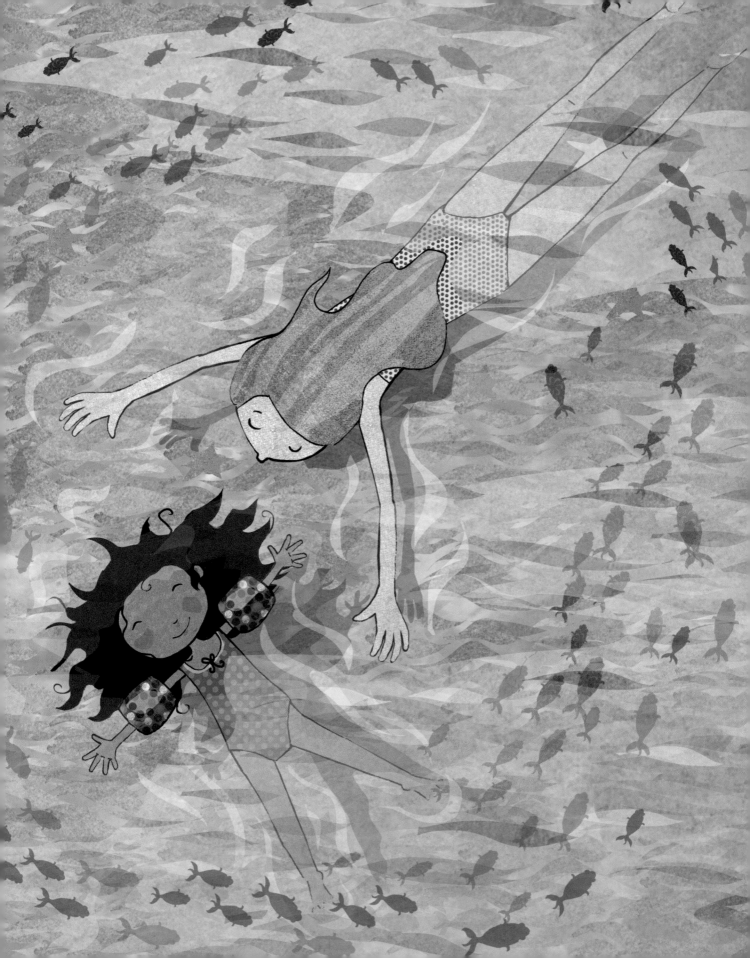

We go to the beach
to see all the blues
and greens of the sea.

My grandma lives in a house
surrounded by the deep colors
of the forest.

Y mi abuela lives in the fast and bright colors of the city.

PIZZA

Colors make the world pretty,
colors make the world interesting and beautiful.

Without them everything would look the same.

People are different colors too. Colors are a part of us. Our colors make us beautiful and unique.

Mommy says it is part of our culture and
the big word diversity—diversidad.

My mommy and daddy look different.
My mommy is the color white, like
crema—cream and has yellow-brown hair.

Her skin turns pink under the sun and
sometimes she gets freckles.

My daddy's skin is brown like smooth leather. He has thick black hair and eyes the color of yummy chocolate! Mmm…que rico chocolate!

My skin is another color. Daddy says café con leche or a mezcla—a mixture of both colors. A color all my own.

We are a colorful,
beautiful, lovely family.

Around us, you can see all the colors of amor—love.

The world is full of hundreds of colors and hundreds and hundreds and hundreds of beautiful families.

Many people can see
the beauty of my family,
and I can see the beauty of their families.

My mommy and daddy look different
and that's not only okay...

It's maravilloso!

Note to Parents and Caregivers

"Love recognizes no barriers. It jumps hurdles, leaps fences, penetrates walls to arrive at its destination full of hope." —Maya Angelou

Marvelous Maravilloso is told from the viewpoint of a little girl, as she navigates the colorful world around her. Her vantage point is particularly special as she comes from a bi-cultural family, and is able to appreciate the differences between her parents, as well as her own unique and beautiful color. As she is coming into her own identity and exploring what this means for her, she comes to appreciate how all families are uniquely beautiful.

This book highlights the wonder a child has in their immediate environment, and the joy that they find in color all around them. Likewise, there are ways that you as a parent or caregiver can help your child appreciate all the ways that diversity makes the world beautiful.

How Children Understand Skin Color[1]

Children begin to notice and respond to skin color cues around six months of age; however, at this age, they do not yet attach the concept of skin color to cultural or racial categories. In the early years, children identify skin color as more of a descriptive factor of the individual.

Around the age of three to four, children begin to identify and group people according to "racial" physical characteristics, but in more generalized terms. They may not understand complexities within these general groups; for example, a child this age may not understand that two people with the same color skin can belong to different cultural or racial groups. They can understand that skin has the same scientific purpose for everyone, regardless of the color of their skin.

By three years of age, a child is starting to be exposed to media, school, community settings, and other influences outside of the family. There is evidence that at this age, societal messages begin to affect a child's ideas and beliefs, including the way they feel about themselves and their group identity.

As a child turns five and six years old, messages from the community become more significant in their influence. Children may choose to play only with children of the same gender or children belonging to a similar racial/cultural group. They can understand simple scientific explanations for differences in skin color. They may enjoy learning about the ways their classmates' home cultures are similar to or different from their own.

By age seven to nine, children are establishing group identities, and are more aware of the dynamics of racism. They can understand the harm in stereotyping and name calling. Children this age are able to grasp more complex scientific explanations for skin color, and may demonstrate interest in learning about the history of cultural communities.

---

[1] The information in this section of the note comes from Derman-Sparks, L. (2012). *Stages in children's development of racial/ cultural identity & attitudes* [lecture]. Retrieved from https://www.uua.org/sites/live-new.uua.org/files/documents/derman-sparkslouise/1206_233_identity_stages.pdf.

How You Can Help

Most children have already identified skin color differences before the adults around them have realized they have. It is developmentally normal for a child to notice differences and have questions about their observations. The following are some guidelines for discussing skin color with your child.

Listen and respond to your child's questions.
The natural response to a child's inquisitive question about a stranger's skin color in the market or on the bus is to respond in a hushed voice, shush the child to talk about it later, or to make a statement that we don't talk about or point at others. This only serves to reinforce that a person's skin color is not something to talk about, admire, or even acknowledge. To a child who was making an observation about their environment, this response is confusing.

What you can do as the parent or caregiver is to positively respond to a child's curious observations. The response can be noticing with them, and pointing out another fact such as the color of the person's dress or cool hat. This acknowledges the child in their study of the environment around them, and supports the positive integration of skin color as a descriptive factor, and not the only identifier in a person's profile.

For example, a child might notice the difference in their skin from their parent, and make the statement "My skin is darker than yours, Mommy, but Daddy's is more brown than mine." A supportive response would be to acknowledge, "You're right, honey, your skin is darker than mine." In this situation there is not a need for added comment, unless the child inquires for more.

Sometimes a child will ask more—the quintessential "why?" question. An example of an appropriate response could be "Your skin is darker than mine because yours is a mixture of my skin color and Daddy's skin color," or a more general statement, such as, "Everyone is unique and has a different skin color, and it is part of a person's beauty. Isn't human nature beautiful?" Sometimes relating in a child-like sense to animals—or another reference your child can relate to—is helpful. For example, you might say something like, "Just like there are many different color kitty cats, there are many different people. You know how our kitty cat is orange with white paws, but the mommy cat where we got him had black patches and some grey mixed with the orange? Skin color is like that, with everyone getting to have their very own, and everyone is beautiful."

Address discrimination—talk about it.
Unfortunately, children can experience negative interactions with others based on race and skin color at very young ages. As a child observes their surroundings, they may witness someone making negative comments or looking hatefully towards someone based on skin color. This can be confusing for the child. If your child witnesses one of these interactions, it is important to listen to their questions and be a role model in how you respond. For example, if your child approaches you after having had one of these experiences and asks about it, a positive response could be, "Unfortunately, some people treat other people unfairly because they are different. In our family we respect everyone and celebrate people's differences." Your child will essentially learn from you as the parent or caregiver what would be the appropriate response.

If perhaps you witness the event with your child and you want to be proactive about it, you can preemptively respond with a general comment, such as the previous example, which might stimulate a conversation with your child. Go with it, and be supportive as they come to understand this in their own developmental terms.

Modeling how to respond to questions about skin color, and countering discrimination are important to help children learn appropriate responses, have respect for others, and to love their own identities. It is especially important for children of bi-cultural backgrounds, as they combine the identity of both cultures into their own sense of self, and think about what these identities could mean for them in the larger society.

It can be hard to talk about differences in skin color, because we are keen on trying to be "politically correct" by not talking about it, or by giving a hushed response as to not offend the person the child is asking about. However, the goal when talking to your child is not to shut down conversation, but to convey that skin color is only a part of who someone is, not the totality of a person.

You are the best resource for helping your child respect and celebrate their own identity and those of others. You are your child's mirror and what you reflect back to them contributes a significant part to their perception of themselves, their identity. You can help your child learn to value their own unique identity, and to find beauty and joy in the differences all around them.

About the Author

Carrie Lara, PsyD, has been working with children in various community mental health settings since 2005. She received her doctorate in clinical psychology from the California School of Professional Psychology through Alliant International University of San Francisco in 2009. Her specializations are working with children and families, child and human development, foster and adoptive youth, learning disabilities and special education, attachment-based play therapy, and trauma. Dr. Lara has had the opportunity to work in different socioeconomic and diverse communities professionally, and personally has a bi-cultural family. Both of these factors have deepened her understanding of the development of cultural identity and its importance. It is her hope that this book supports families having conversations about cultural identity during this very early stage in a child's development of a sense of self.

About the Illustrator

Christine Battuz obtained a master of arts degree from l'Accademia di Belle Arti di Perugia in Italy. Her delightful illustrations can be found in over sixty children's books and magazines.

About Magination Press

Magination Press is an imprint of the American Psychological Association, the largest scientific and professional organization representing psychologists in the United States and the largest association of psychologists worldwide.